I thought we were Post- #MeToo

I thought We were Post-MeToo

Brandy Del Río

Published by Brandy Del Río, 2024.

This is a work of fiction. Similarities to real people, places, or events are entirely coincidental.

I THOUGHT WE WERE POST-METOO

First edition. August 26, 2024.

ISBN: 979-8227796820

Written by Brandy Del Río.

This book is for my mother, father, may he rest peacefully, my brother, as well as, my niece and nephew.

Thank you.

A collection of poems
by Brandy del Río

BRANDY DEL RÍO

© 2024 by Brandy Del Rio. All rights reserved.

Published by Pichoro Inc., South Carolina, 29102 United States

First Edition

Library of Congress Cataloging-in-Publication Data:

Printed in United States

Cover design and editing by Brandy Del Rio and Pichoro Inc.

You have a voice worth hearing

3

This book has been edited to provide context and further information about many of the events that actually happened.

Introduction

Something that has come to me many times in the past year is the image of the dragonfly. When doing research for this book, I found that dragonflies have been used by many cultures as symbols of those who have passed on. I am a pensive person and I would like to think that this is true.

To some, the strange animal resembling an alien creature with wings and large bulbous eyes, they are a symbol for prosperity on a path and new beginnings. I'm constantly visited by these creatures when I sit and do my writing on the back porch. It's a place that has somehow become abandoned since my father passed. But it's like they are cheering me on and encouraging me to finish the project. Honestly, I like to think that. My mother has butterflies. I have dragonflies.

I could spew off facts about the origin of the dragonfly, its natural habitat, weight and size, diet and common colors, but that would be boring.
And this book is not about dragonflies.

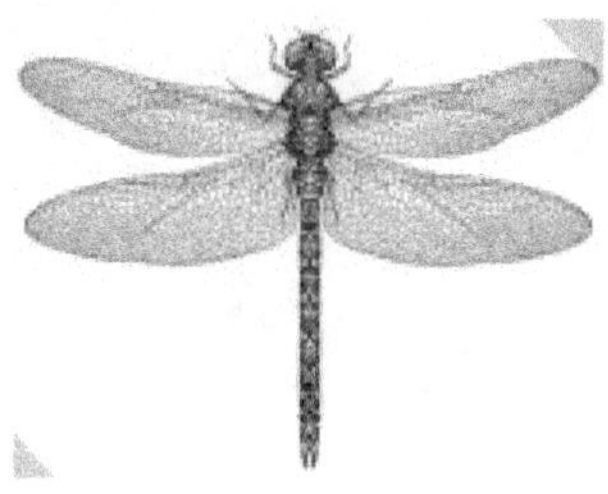

She set out in search

I THOUGHT WE WERE POST-METOO

Where the bumble bee goes to die

quiet
unassuming
soft warm ground
she buzzes
until just right
then
slowly she lands
humming softly
quiet

BRANDY DEL RÍO

The Second Born

the truck with no charge
take a spin
I was the motor, the push
with all loose wires under invisible hood

over lumpy solid lawn
patches of green and yellow
amber clay rocks where we built
the castles of our dreams

ups and downs and round the bend
more bumps on the ride
he asked
faster

I told him
to steer to the rocky, unlevel ground
the space where we always dug
our castles of clay

giggles then
a small dip
and with a light thud
and a flip
laughing with the shock and thrill
Then, crying
he was so young and always cried
I came around the turned over miniature auto

I THOUGHT WE WERE POST-METOO

Silken amber on powder like the beginnings of a cake
the perfect gash aligned with his eyebrow
from empty hood
run to tell God that Abel was struck

BRANDY DEL RÍO

When the child fell ill

I remember the time where the ditch was full to the brim
a cup of tea without the cream
in front of the house
the rain never let up and the owls were
hoo-hooing in the trees

The window always slightly ajar let out the voices
yells of all those who lived there
Screams from the women who only did as they were told
begged for forgiveness

Drunken sneers from the men
that came home demanding
silver platter and spoon
polish for their boots

children were outside
always
running and providing their own symphony

Why be in the cacophony of frustration and guilt in the shabby shack?

Four walls of wood
chipped paint
heavy sentiment

one man outside
sober
With the feverish child swaddled in pink and white

I THOUGHT WE WERE POST-METOO

pale and glistening from the fever
ear stuffed with some cotton
and ointment

this was refuge

BRANDY DEL RÍO

*Tornado off of I 95**

The cyclone touched down, and it took
everything but the front porch
blocks of cinder from the foundation
knocked out the windows
and only frames were left to see
of the remains
dilapidated wood frame
left of the house that once sat there

eerie orange sky

It could have taken
those steps away

the blocks were steadfast
Unmoving, constant
and something that would stay
to be seen by their grandchildren
It was a flurry of dust now that
the torment had passed
What could be described by many was only felt by few
but the tumble weeds were only noticed in the quiet
Wind blowing
them into the distance

now
we pick up
move on

I THOUGHT WE WERE POST-METOO

Making Tortillas

Circles of water, charcos
Burbujas they used to say when you were in kindergarten
or maybe it was something that your Gram used to mutter when she was
fixing her tortillas

The flour in its bowl
baking powder, levadura for fluffy malleable pieces
soft and not cracker-like
She used to call it something Spanish like
eh-*spow-daaahh*

      but con acento

A pinch of salt for flavor
and with your hands you mix
Run the tiny grains between your fingers to make sure the flavor is
through it
but really *through* it

Boil water but heat it up just enough
to have some steam rise when you pour
and don't be afraid to get your hands hot
they won't burn
with your fingers in the powder make a hole, un hueco
A crater-like form in the middle
and then pour
but don't use all of the liquid

with your fingers make a doughy mixture

be careful to knead with love
for the husband for whom you will bear fruit
Respect for the parents that raised you
Joy that can be felt by your children to be

Form the orbs you will roll flat with the pin that can crater the ground

El palote

A stick to swat the flies that will eventually come in to
grab one with mantequilla
Once flat cook on a cast iron plate

El comal
Watch like a hawk so as not to waste a whole batch
of maybe bread
Burnt spots are an acquired taste
not everyone likes them
but I do
Stack them and wrap them with a cloth
They could become that hardened cracker
if you leave them
Enjoy them before they do

I THOUGHT WE WERE POST-METOO

When you grow up the daughter of an immigrant

It sometimes feels like

As a child you are an inconvenience to everyone
You don't draw attention to yourself
because you are drawing attention to them
and everyone in tow to include your aunts, and uncles, grandmas and
cousins

Gas is not cheap
and you aren't going to pay for any car
expenses or repairs
on the preowned
Ford Explorer

I am a Mexican American
and my Texican mother is fairer than
Thin sliced Sunbeam bread
She was born fair
and stayed that way
not like me
cause I was born the perfect shade
of lightly baked dough
the kind that the Pillsbury doughboy flaunted
before he would "huh-hoo" his way to fame

You know you are different from the start
'Cause you grow up thinking that everyone
speaks Spanglish and has brown skin
until you step into a McDonald's in another place

to see the first black man in your life
and freeze, because everyone you had seen
before was a lighter shade of brown

you hear your grandma tell the story and laugh
she doesn't think anything of it
because everyone in her life has always been brown
in different shades
according to the job they could get
and the wage they would be paid
the lightness of the foundation
they could buy
at the drug store

sometimes you envy the rubias on tv
the girls with sunshine locks and hair
that does not kink when you brush it when it is dry
or that is stick straight like Marcia Brady

the women in the gringa salons
do not know how to treat your hair
without ruining every follicle to fried hell
you grow up hating it until
a friend of your mom's lends her a straightening iron
I am a Latina who has always known
that I won't be good enough
due to lack of education and religiosity
Sexism from the cradle
and an echoing call from Cortes and his henchmen

but
I hear her and know the truth

I THOUGHT WE WERE POST-METOO

That those things are just not true
because Doña Marina was smart enough to learn three languages
and replace a religious man who was appointed his personal translator
and that makes her the ultimate incarnation of evil
because she knew how to use her gifts
to sway a pale Spanish man to gift her a space as his confidante

and you are just as smart

hija

de la Malinche*

Made little notice of fools

I THOUGHT WE WERE POST-METOO

The Boy with the excuses

The boy with the excuses is never at fault
he lost his last job because his coworkers were too old did not appreciate
his youthful spirit
he sits and ruminates over things
that have long since passed

The boy with the excuses returns to a serving job
at a restaurant
all of the people in town know him by name
he sits and ponders what he can possibly do next

The boy with the excuses lets his friends find out
by text message that he has attempted suicide
He walks through his house
floor littered with the remains of a season of habit
he shouldn't be bothered by cleaning

The boy with the excuses goes to a gas station
gets beer as a freebie
the owner knew his father
the sheriff got him out of a few tight situations
with his help
the boy bids the owner thanks and is on his way
for another night of drunken antics

The boy with the excuses sleeps until noon
wakes with an ache in his shoulder blade; it's sharp
he can't put two and two together

that rolling around in bed for the entirety of the day could possibly cause
aches and pains
he also can't recall the events of last night

The boy with the excuses sleeps in after a pleasant night with friends
he has acquired the very bad habit of not locking his front door
he also doesn't respond to his former girlfriend's messages
he says she is crazy

The boy with the excuses wakes to his crazy ex
treating him like a punching bag
he is face down on the bed
not knowing how she made it in
and what her problem is now

it's her fault
she has the problem, not him

The boy with the excuses wraps his arm across
his lover's back
reaches for her forearm and gently caresses it
he profusely apologizes for the antics that just played
in his untidy and unlocked room just minutes ago
he says it doesn't bother him
his eyes tell a different story
he can't take responsibility for the fact that he messed up
and he keeps messing up.

I THOUGHT WE WERE POST-METOO

Adventurous girlfriend

I once was asked to be an adventurous girlfriend
by a guy who felt he needed to prove himself
he posed in front of his bathroom mirror and flexed
the adventurous part was that he wanted a" girlfriend" who would participate
in what they call a Daisy chain

He wanted to be sexually gratified by being able to say he had the experience
of having sex with a girl and a guy at the same time
he then sent me a video of him being penetrated
by another man
all I could think was why?
Why did he feel he could openly send
videos and pictures
on to someone he really didn't know.
It was the audacity to solicit that left me aghast
Is he serious?
Why did he feel okay with this?
But then I landed on the answer

The simple fact that He was a he
and I a She
the blatant privilege that goes unrecognized by so many
and he pressed unapologetically as if I owed
him anything because he came to me
and opened up about these desires
It hurts my heart to think he found a poor She
who only wanted to be accommodating
or maybe reckless in her own regard

maybe She too was told that this was her role in life
to appease men
maybe she just didn't question the circumstances
and maybe He was suffering his own confusion
that it was not right in society's eyes
to be open to love from both genders
So, it had to be concealed

I THOUGHT WE WERE POST-METOO

12:43

a brisk dark
night
a step out onto
a 3rd floor balcony

glance up
and the only warmth
was that from the light
escaping from the open

window in the loft
They shared
Although they were no longer
Together

The still air cut his face
on the way
to the ground
if you blink

and the clock changes
to 12:44
you will have missed him
alive

BRANDY DEL RÍO

Honey I'm home

Latin men like to get home and have dinner ready
it's an expectation ingrained in their psyche from a very early age
like when my grandmother married my grandfather
she fixed beans not knowing that she had to steep the legumes in water
before cooking
consequently, they were thrown at her the first week
of their marriage
that incident would not arrive again
except for occasional alcohol fueled tantrums
on days when he was dealing with his unprocessed trauma

They expect the children to be home and cared for
before they arrive so they can galivant with their masculine, but demure,
stance
and coax women into illicit affairs that they never knew they wanted
but would quickly be replaced by the next pretty little minx that entered
the restaurant
Like my aunt's husband before the eternal divorce

They want there to be a meal prepared when they get home from a long
day at work
like my mother everyday of her marriage with my father
except for those days when she worked late
which was most nights before the second Bush entered office
she got off for elections and most federal holidays
went home to pots of sticky noodles

Because it is not his job to clean them
because he shouldn't have to know how make a formidable meal
because he should be able to do what he wants

I THOUGHT WE WERE POST-METOO

but not her
never her because she will look like
she is inviting anyone to do something to her

because her body is not her own

BRANDY DEL RÍO

A boy who thought he was a man

A boy who thought he was a man
would only show up when he was drunk
or had taken a hit of his special stuff
'Cause his plug was his best friend

Baby he would call me
Baby
Baby
Baby

He would show up with his speakers booming
playing music that I couldn't possibly know
his voice would blunder down the hall
I'd know it from the moment he turned the corner
always on his phone
Exotifying music from a distant culture because it felt good
He would later don those stereotypical accents
in a not so ironic way

We carried on for some time
and I would always be reminded that I had to impress
Everyone
That his friends didn't like me, and his mother probably wouldn't either
because he was the only child of a woman who normalized the bullshit
she was handed
A story not so uncommon
because that is what women sometimes do
His father was an alcoholic who learned how to not be sober
but still get the service done
Who spread his seed in every military base he set foot in

I THOUGHT WE WERE POST-METOO

The Boy would try every chemical disposable to man
I never knew the real Boy
Who reminded me of my own father
in his bravado and behavior
If only because that is what addicts do
to never have to face the shit that they are handed
but never able to process

BRANDY DEL RÍO

I was never a first generation anything

my dad was always American
when he placed two feet
on Texan soil he was more gringo
than the men he came to work for
minimum wage that eventually got negotiated
after he watched enough episodes of
Miami Vice and Law and Order
I sat next to him when the Grito
was summoned and he just frowned
almost embarrassed that it was tradition
Tradición que es ridículo

my mom was always American
her fair skin and angular features
always screamed European
never did her parents recognize
anything that was not Spanish
she was stunning
her love for blue jeans and high-top sneakers
hair that reached heaven with Aquanet
she was a phlebotomist with a passion
for bodybuilding and muscles
a love for Slippery When Wet

my mother was the first to receive a degree
my father was the first to get a presidential pardon*

they married and raised my brother and me

I THOUGHT WE WERE POST-METOO

we are what they were striving for

though I do not feel American

BRANDY DEL RÍO

Aquí

Aquí me encuentro en la silla
sólo mis pensamientos me acompañan
son tristes
Sin embargo, los tengo

los pensamientos de que quizás
no voy a encontrar mi lugar
este mundo no valora lo que yo tengo
ya me lo ha dicho en varias ocasiones

No es mi lugar para dirigir a los demás
una gente que gobierna como si mañana
ya fuera permanente
que ya se nos ha dado a seres
humanos

Los días son regalos para disfrutar
pero en este tiempo, no se sabe
tal vez nunca se ha sabido
y en estos tiempos no creo que hemos aprendido

salgo al jardín para hablar con mis amigos:
las habas, los pájaros, los chapulines
que me acompañan para contarme chismes
que la tierra no está feliz

tal vez yo no soy feliz tampoco
la siguiente página de mi vida se ha cambiado
nada está seguro

I THOUGHT WE WERE POST-METOO

y no sé qué hacer con esta energía

BRANDY DEL RÍO

A Fateless Job

when a boss invites you to a discussion table
you are to be seen
not heard
you give your thoughts and feel their eyes

when their boss leaves
for repercussions from
inappropriate conduct
you keep your thoughts but feel their eyes

you are there for a check
for the line on your CV
one step closer
to middle of the road

This isn't your endgame
but it sometimes seems
as if this is what you are supposed
to aspire to

sometimes there is a string
of many of these
humdrum roles
they can drag you down
but if you keep your eyes
steady on the point
where you'd like to be
you might break away

I THOUGHT WE WERE POST-METOO

Dark Man
In conversation with Dr. Clarissa Pinkola Estés' 'dark man'

I know him
He lingers in the corner with every thought I produce
"But you can't" he whispers
With syrup spraying with every syllable
You can't get far because you have to help me
and I pause and get nowhere.
He says I'm ridiculous because I express myself with words he doesn't like
because he doesn't understand them
It never occurs to him to break out of his box made of plywood
and manicured turf that never grows past
an inch
He swats at me when I get too close to leaving

and then I catch a fleeting glimpse
in the mirror of my eyes
He is me with sunken hollow cheeks

You are not supposed to get anywhere
I hiss in a voice from a dream
a memory long forgotten

I have been here before

BRANDY DEL RÍO

Aren't they all

once I was in a relationship with a boy
who discounted mental health
or psychiatry

after a few weeks of dating,
I stopped taking my medication
my sleep aide
supposed mood stabilizer
I had been taking 5 years

It was something
I didn't really put much thought into it

I was, as I have come to learn,
dickmatized

He came
in with feigned enlightenment
A reiki healer
supreme meditator
he had this way of making things
seem less intimidating

my parents loved him
with his learned tongue
generous pocket
throwing the dime
and hoity explanation
because I could not possibly know anything

I THOUGHT WE WERE POST-METOO

I stopped liking him really quickly
now I realize he was just a distraction

BRANDY DEL RÍO

Escape

I could smell him before I saw him
slumped on the seat in front of the television
watching whatever nonsensical program one watches
to dull the monotony of the everyday rhythm
that makes sense in the time that you are not toiling away
and breaking your neck to make a hard day's wage

He didn't know anything else in his own upbringing
He thought his mother was his aunt for the first
fourteen years of his life
and his grandmother was the only coddling arm
he would know in his life

he swam a river to break the chains
only to be summoned back in time to let his own children know
their blood born grandmother

though she did not care
to form a bond with them, either

Like the burning of Cuauhtémoc's feet
by the savage Cortés
even though Hernan was the civil one
the savage wore paint
for the battle and feared not when the ships landed

Cuauhtémoc* could not run for the flames and armor

The drunken man ran away to a different place that did not want him

I THOUGHT WE WERE POST-METOO

where he had to pretend to be someone else
a place that legends of vaqueros seemed attainable

he would mold
his own children to desire to be
the best puffed chest scoundrels
of good name and reputation.
This was his job well done
A nation was made proud and a legacy remained

BRANDY DEL RÍO

The Willow

Long vines of leaves for play
The jester calling for the princess
as winds waft
in the aromas
of broken grass
Three no longer cherubs
and bubbly giggles
guarded by a sturdy trunk of wood

Soon
wind blows away the laughter
with the light hair of the princess
The dragons of time and season
take her
and their innocent eyes never meet again

I THOUGHT WE WERE POST-METOO

Emotionally unavailable man

I spot you in your place of work
I accidentally offend you

You understand this take my comments with grace
I see the way you look
but you are engulfed in your work

That my dear makes you more appealing

I recognize that you are a man possessed by your work
frankly, that's more interesting
my cross to bear

BRANDY DEL RÍO

Another savior complex

Congratulations
you used your
Non platform
to convince

millions
you are a Christ-like figure

to clarify
You are Not
Never have been
Never was

but the myth
will build
and prevail
as will the stolen

fist in the air
because it was not
your symbol
yet another thing you stole no credit will be given

we will sink
into this Gilead

suffer the consequence of a public
pandering to a toddler
who embodies

I THOUGHT WE WERE POST-METOO

the bigotry

BRANDY DEL RÍO

Karen sleeps

My friend Karen sleeps well at night
because she makes herself oblivious to the events happening in the world
it does not affect her
so, she dismisses it while she buys another overpriced yoga mat and a
water bottle to match
the interior of her car

She bought this car with the money from her job
got her degree in business
learned just enough to secure a job that she openly complains about
having to work
40 hours a week
exerts minimal mental energy and spends her free time
browsing the internet looking for new hobbies
she has none that she has come to on her own
it's too hard to decide for herself

the comforts of upper-class living are too much not to live with, so she
buys more
she complains that welfare should not be a thing
her taxes are paying for that
she is the authority on all things business and finance
does not understand how some people
don't make better investments
like buying instead of renting
it does not occur to her that there are people out there with more
priorities than just themselves and they live paycheck to paycheck
caring for family and parents
that never let them go hungry
money gets tight

but people should want to learn because she taught herself so many things by watching
videos on the internet
She doesn't know that there are some who do not have access to the luxuries
she takes for granted
like high-speed internet that is never compromised
by faulty wiring or proximity to the nearest city

she does not bother herself with the state of politics because she doesn't need to know
when a man cannot condone white supremacy
and bigotry
it is none of her business
she is not affected
All of her friends should be the same homogeneous flavor of bland
that is completely disconnected from modern times
because any passion is displaced

and the status quo should not be tampered with
It will just disrupt her hot yoga schedule

Learned to be human

I THOUGHT WE WERE POST-METOO

White Girl

I was 20 years old
when I first recall
a white girl
referring to me
as La Gringa at a Mexican restaurant

It was stupid
and a ridiculous
generalization after we
seemingly bonded
over Mexican film

who doesn't like Gael and Diego
and their partnering roles

I just laughed it off
at that dinner table
as she was older than me

She was the friend
of two other girls
I had befriended
a year before
I thought it rude
to not accept
this seemingly dismissive
comment about me and my identity

It wasn't the first time

that I paid into
played into stereotypes

when in gringolandia,
you have to cater to a watered down
image of what that latinidad
is supposed to look like

Most often it does not make sense

I THOUGHT WE WERE POST-METOO

Aren't we post #MeToo?*

To think many still think ill of women
We don't have something in our blood
that makes us the movers of all bad things in the world
despite what some may say

We are beautiful
majestic creatures of God
your creator
or just biology;
I won't assume to impose a belief on you

unlike the patriarchy before me

Society

Constantine

Alexander

Washington

Jefferson
Napoleon in his naval fleet

Caesar and his chariots

King Henry the 8th killed his wives not knowing
his little swimmers were the culprit
of not having a son

But always the woman

the root of all evil

Porn is your sex education?
Fast pumping does not please a woman
When it's okay to call a girl a slut
because she likes to flirt
but a boy screws anything that moves
some call him a stud
Can we please clarify that double standard?

When I have to go down a list of great world leaders
to number 16 to find Queen Elizabeth I
but Trumpito
with this pussy grabbing
gets in at number 10
It shows what is really valued

The day when a man can walk
with blood dripping from his privates
stand the pain that prepares our wombs for labor

When he can walk into a bar
be hit on by some drunk, awkward guy
who can't even string a sentence together

    and hold it together

The question is answered by many of these behaviors

I THOUGHT WE WERE POST-METOO

We aren't through #MeToo

We are still in the middle of it

BRANDY DEL RÍO

Ways to evade a Panic Attack

Patience
and resilience

Breathe in
Breathe out

Get out of bed

Stand up
Stretch and reach for the heavens

and walk around

drink water

Go outside

Repeat.

I THOUGHT WE WERE POST-METOO

I feel like the sky today

Gray and weepy
it's frightening

painful

heavy clouds
they carry away secrets

with the wind
they waft away

BRANDY DEL RÍO

An attempt at meditation

close eyes
hands
in lap
spine

so
Straight

Breathe

calm
and counted

but only for the in and out
maybe?

tall
chin down
no thought

and clear patient in the blank

only stomach
moving
in and out

with Breath

Collapse

I THOUGHT WE WERE POST-METOO

Candle

I received you in my visions as I lay asleep
You were happy and mute in those dreams
Your skin was brown
stained red from the day's labor
when you ventured past the four-post bed

You lay there, I would approach
If only to kiss you on the forehead
being the lone lamb to visit the shepherd
for fear of the staff to turn to a whip like the hand that fed them

When you did leave
many came to receive you
You lay limp in the frame that had little but sheets
my breathing was labored as if I had the tumors in my lungs

it was the first time I received the dead
felt the presence of the world past the veil
I was made to embrace that halo of light,
and I welcomed it

BRANDY DEL RÍO

Maybe you knew I was to fall ill then.
You knew that I would be struck limp and forced
to live with a cross to bear, not live the life beyond
what their illusions let them see

I was not what they wanted for so long
but neither were you
When Vela lit her candles like her name,
she did not understand
The power and magic behind the flame
in her action
the last breath lit her candle

I THOUGHT WE WERE POST-METOO

Altar

The altar sits in a corner
adorned more ornately
than a Catholic church
she puts pictures of saints she venerates
lights the candles with empty words
they are supposed to go up to an almighty white man really, it's just an oversize
picture of a scantily clad Santa Claus or Zeus
Orville Redenbacher or the General Mills oat tin

She keeps the pictures
of some loved ones that have passed on
some borrowed photos and prayer cards from funerals
pictures that have been discarded
with old candles that are a safety hazard
when she insists on leaving them on

She finds miniature
figures of saints to stick on the table
once she put a piece of used chewing gum
on the bottom of the figures to make it stay
here is where she keeps her collection
of rosary beads that she never pulls out the drawer

there are also mini bottles of holy water that she refills every single time
she goes to chapel
Every other suggestion of God is negated by her upbringing
dogma
professed faith
altar with the votive candles

shrine
for
to
by God

I THOUGHT WE WERE POST-METOO

Perfect

I don't understand this obsession with the perfect look
It has existed for as long as people
could obsess over looks
this crafting and piecing
the perfect features together
plastic surgery
Alterations
to skin
cheeks
eye and lip

the curve and shape
a natural hip

Plumping of rear
to accentuate a tiny waist
all to look better
to the naked eye

No other benefits
maybe indirectly
Not purposefully

Take out that fat
put it right here
Make me smoother
The perfect curve

Fix this crook

BRANDY DEL RÍO

Make this go away

Filters are fake
They offer up the unreal

Photoshop takes away
the perfection of imperfection

But I like the natural me
if I don't subscribe to this body hate
What does that say about me?

That there isn't anything wrong with me

I THOUGHT WE WERE POST-METOO

As for me

I learned to have meaningless relations
I had no real type
I only knew that they
had to have a relatively pretty face
to look at
Be able to carry a conversation
That was not filled with social media references
and hot button topics

I was alone

Mejor sola qué mal compañada

Better alone than in bad company

It is what I have gotten used to,

although, I still hope for tomorrow

BRANDY DEL RÍO

Silla Vacía

con la silla vacía
recordemos todo

decía que los verdaderos amigos son
los que te ayudan cuando
estás en la cárcel o estas enfermo

y así es
con la silla vacía
a el fin de la mesa

a la cabecera de la mesa

son pocos que vinieron
pero así se siente mejor

I THOUGHT WE WERE POST-METOO

Ode to the Mockingbird

You small gray soft fluff
who dwells beneath the canopy of trees
you scrape and gather around
in time when the weather is just warm enough
to gather and build your home for the season;

you do this for survival
because it is innate
it is in you to make sure
your line will exist
because you can

you sing with your brethren to tell tales
of your adventures
the things you have seen
What you have heard
and gossip of the unmentionables

Like the house that sits at the base of the land
Where forgotten children dwell,
the ones who will never be reclaimed
They came to live here because their parents did not care
to help them anymore

You saw the empty box with the broken windows down the street
where things not spoken occur
the small bags passed in exchange for currency

there dwells the exotic transportation that moves

with only seconds to spare
because here deep in the land there is no time to spare
in the pursuit of experience

From your nests you peer all of the happenings
and hear the car horns from the inpatient
They need to get to the next destination
because only they exist in this place separate
from all of the hustle of cities

I THOUGHT WE WERE POST-METOO

*Ojos de pichoro**
Porque me cantan
siempre cuando salgo para fuera
siempre tan alto

con esos ojos de pichoro

es regalo de más allá
y mensaje
que vamos ha estar bien

BRANDY DEL RÍO

We are community

we gravitate to each other
clique with others
that resemble us
it is home

we see our friends
at church or community events
sit with them

they speak with accentuation
often gesticulating
the movements are grande

Caramel skin with darker tones
the darker ones are picked last
like kids on the school playground

we go to the new restaurant
where they hired a lady
to make handmade tortillas

we go to the same gossip circle
where they once trashed
Your brother's and sister's good name
we marry the guy
with the crooked face
or the man with adult braces
and acne because he won't hurt a fly

I THOUGHT WE WERE POST-METOO

when the man balls his fist
shows you the inside of his palm
it's ok because you know this danger

this violence is familiar
you know how to fight it
and you are ok with the familiar
as long as you keep it within the family

more for Tía Tita to bring to her sewing table

community

your face is in the window

i.
your face is in the window
It will forever be there
Imprinted on this place
It will not lose your pictured grace

The trees you dug and covered in the ground
waft in the breeze so desperate
For reception into a face
that yearns to be lilted with the leaves

I sat there as you took your last breath
embraced my mother as she wept
thank you for waiting for me
to finally let go of your body

because it wasn't yours anymore
a cavern for the malignancy
you fought to burn
while it scorched your skin

I THOUGHT WE WERE POST-METOO

ii.
I sat there
as they
inappropriately came to me with complaints
about your manner of being

But that's the thing
That moment was not
the time nor the place to complain
about someone's existence

not caring about the way that they felt
about my father
I didn't care about whatever grievances
Were held against Him

That is not my business
No time to allow space for me to grieve
for us closest to him to mourn
allowing grace for that would be too much to ask for

iii.
I listened as my mother recounted
how his family who never visited
or came to see him while he was sick
Inquired about his insurance policy

As if they would be named the beneficiaries
I was there when they called and showed up
At my parents' home expecting for someone to offer an empty room
the night before his funeral

Remember how the one sister called him on his deathbed exclaiming
how she forgave him for everything
When the same sister was in the procession to get lunch after the mass
and exclaimed that it was what she came for when they finally served the
food

the aunt who came and sat with the long-face
in the second pew in front of the altar
taking care of my hat while secretly stealing my prayer card
but you were never fond of her

I THOUGHT WE WERE POST-METOO

iv.
I am here when they remember
Pop Pop is in the trees
The firewood that will lay there
Rot over time

The mancave that will remain locked
Stuffed with his favorite things
the projects that will remain unfinished
the salvageables that remained in the icebox

The landscaping that made the yard
so much more bearable even though it largely will remain untouched
but you never did it for anyone else
because working the earth made you feel good

Remember
man,
that you are dust,
and to dust you shall return.

BRANDY DEL RÍO

Dear Peter Pan

you fly so high
Never coming down to reign in each night
They keep stretching out so you never have to sleep
you search and your mind never gains a peep

You find a new Wendy to take back to Neverland
thinking she will rock you fro and back
Sing to you and clean up after you when you have a mess at hand

But did you ask if she wanted to come
For Tinkerbell isn't one to share
your company seems crowded with dear Michael
and John
After all Lost boys do need a mom

That star that is number two on the right and straight on
till morning and the peaking of dawn
it's where they go to evade time
There it shall sit until eyes touch the line

The trials of today will grow to no end
and then they shall return once again
So make room my dear you will need space
for the extra mouths need their place

Notes:

- In 2005, a tornado touched down on a small community named Winters Hill. No one died. Some family friends of ours were displaced. I was 15 years old.

- La Malinche was a real person. Her name was Doña Marina and she became the unofficial translator for Hernán Cortés when he came seeking gold in what is now Mexico. She is the mother of the Mestizo race in Mexico. She was an Aztec woman who garnered the favor of the conquistador. Like many women in history, she has a fairly contentious reputation. To many Mexicans she is a traitor. Since the beginning of written Mexican history, it has been taught that Malinche sold out the Aztec empire to the Spanish conquistadors. In all reality, we weren't there so we don't actually know what happened. Nevertheless, she has a negative reputation in Mexican history. This has been perpetuated by many different institutions like the Catholic Church and the Spanish government. She is often portrayed as a co-conspirator with Cortés.

- In 1986, President Ronald Reagan signed a bill into law granting Amnesty for over 3 million undocumented immigrants who had been in the United States since before 1982. My father was one of those people.

- In 1986, President Ronald Reagan signed a bill into law granting Amnesty for over 3 million undocumented immigrants who had been in the United States since before 1982. My father was one of those people.

- *Women Who Run with the Wolves: Myths and Stories of the Wild* Woman is a must read for all women who do not necessarily fit into the molds that are set forth by society. I learned so much from this read.

- Cuauhtémoc was the Aztec prince and Moctezuma's son at the time of the Spanish conquest of Mexico. He was a brave and still work force and he is said to have been a great warrior for the Aztec empire. He captured and tortured and subsequently bound with his feet being burned.

- A Pichoro is a type of bird. My great aunt used to talk about these birds that resided in the trees in South Texas.

References:

Aboulhosn, Angelica, et al. "La Malinche, Hernán Cortés's Translator and so Much More." *National Endowment for the Humanities*, www.neh.gov/article/la-malinche-hernan-cortess-translator-and-so-much-more.

Legalization (Amnesty) for Unauthorized Immigrants", *Debates on U.S. Immigration*, Thousand Oaks, California: Sage Publications, Inc., pp. 53–74, 2012

US Department of Commerce, NOAA. "Tornadoes of 2005." *National Weather Service*, NOAA's National Weather Service, 23 Aug. 2016, www.weather.gov/lmk/tornado_climatology_2005[1].

Legalization (Amnesty) for Unauthorized Immigrants"[2], *Debates on U.S. Immigration*, Thousand Oaks, California: Sage Publications, Inc., pp. 53–74, 2012

Estés, Clarissa Pinkola. *Women Who Run with the Wolves: Myths and Stories of the Wild Woman Archetype*. Rider, 2022.

Mojica Rodríguez, Prisca Dorcas. *For Brown Girls with Sharp Edges and Tender Hearts: A Love Letter to Women of Color*. SEAL, 2021.

---

1. http://www.weather.gov/lmk/tornado_climatology_2005

2. https://dx.doi.org/10.4135/9781452218489.n4

About the Author

Brandy Del Rio is a writer with a deep passion for feminism and all things Hispanic history. She loves the food and is a proud heritage speaker